**What was Indiana Jones doing
down South in spring 1913?**

Indiana Jones is that world-famous, whip-cracking hero you know from the movies....

But was he *always* cool and fearless in the face of danger? Did he *always* get mixed up in hair-raising, heart-stopping adventures?

Yes!

Read all about Indy as a kid....Watch him solve a mystery that stretches from South Carolina to Boston....And get ready for some nonstop, edge-of-your-seat excitement!

Young Indiana Jones books

YOUNG INDIANA JONES™

and the
PLANTATION TREASURE

By William McCay

Random House 🏠 New York

Young Indy novels are conceived and produced by Random House, Inc.,
in conjunction with Lucasfilm Ltd.

Library of Congress Cataloging-in-Publication Data
McCay, William.
    Young Indiana Jones and the plantation treasure.
    Summary: In the spring of 1913, fourteen-year-old Indiana Jones traces the
route of the Underground Railroad to help a young woman find her family
fortune, lost before the Civil War.
    [1. Underground railroad—Fiction. 2. Buried treasure—Fiction.
3. Adventure and adventurers—Fiction] I. Title.
PZ7.M4784136Yo 1990 [Fic] 89-43388
ISBN 0-679-80579-6 (pbk.) 0-679-90579-0 (lib. bdg.)

Manufactured in the United States of America   4 5 6 7 8 9 0

YOUNG INDIANA JONES

and the

PLANTATION TREASURE

The Beginning

The oil lamp sent flickering shadows dancing around the library walls of Ravenall Hall. The owner of the house, Ashley Ravenall, stood by the French windows. Outside, the sunset painted the cotton fields of his South Carolina plantation a bright orange.

Sighing, he turned to his desk. He picked up the pen lying across his journal. Dipping it into an inkwell, he began to write.

September 13, 1858
Ravenall Hall

I did not wish to take up my pen today. Yet I feel I must record the news that came in. Lawyer Harkwood down in Charleston finally replied to my letter. The story is not pretty.

Harkwood's agents purchased seventy bales of cotton, six hogsheads of molasses, and two slaves from my plantation. The records of my overseer, Harlan Clegg, show no such sales. This confirms my suspicions. Clegg is a thief.

Ravenall leaned back in his seat, rubbing his eyes. Then he went back to writing.

I must find out how much more Clegg has stolen. I fear I made it all too easy for him. In the year since my wife died, I have not set my mind to business. Oh, Elizabeth! How could I think of everyday things with you gone? But I must put aside sorrow, and work for the future. Clegg may have stolen our cotton. But his hands will never touch our family fortune.

Our wealth must be passed on to the Ravenalls of the future. I have already taken steps to make that happen. In spite of Clegg's insisting that I buy more slaves, I have kept the money from our excellent harvest. It will go into wise investments. Mills, railroads . . . so many new companies. In years to come, these will support my sons and let me do the right thing for my black working people. Elizabeth and I talked of it many times. Now I'll do it. When I die, all my slaves shall be set free.

Some may call me foolish, a traitor to the South. Yet I cannot believe we do ourselves any good, staying on this mad course. We live on the labor of human beings. We call them property. We buy and sell them. Yet we fall behind the rest of the country. Now we even threaten to break the Union of these United States. And all because of slavery.

My plan is clear. It is written down in the draft of my will. My family will be protected—no matter what.

Ravenall sighed. Then, once more, he set pen to paper.

My poor young sons! There will be money for them if I pass away before my time. But I fear Clegg may get his hands on the money that should be theirs. I have hidden my investments with the letters from Harkwood. Only I know where they are.

After this evening, Dexter Fairburn, my lawyer in town, will know, too. He will become the guardian of my secret, and of the Ravenall fortune.

Ravenall slipped a bundle of papers into his pocket. Then he went back to his journal.

> Now I need to teach the young ones. The clue to their future will always be in front of them. But they must know where to look.

Ravenall smiled at the thought.

> They must learn. If Papa dies, they must ask Harriet Robinson, the young kitchen slave, about Treasure.

Still smiling, Ravenall shut the journal. When closed, it looked like a regular book. Its green leather binding matched a set of books on the library shelves. There were even gold letters on the spine, spelling out a title. *"The Sermons of Cotton Mather,"* Ravenall read aloud. "Harlan Clegg's not the kind to read the sayings of a preacher. Especially a Yankee preacher."

He slipped the disguised journal into an empty space on a bookshelf. "Just one more book in the library," he muttered.

Then, tapping the draft of the will in his pocket, he stepped into the hall. "Thomas!" Ravenall called. "Is my horse ready? I'm off to see Lawyer Fairburn."

Moments later, Ashley Ravenall stepped through the French doors and onto his horse.

He hurried off for his appointment—an appointment he never kept.

Chapter 1

"I hate straw hats," young Indiana Jones grumbled as he walked down the street. He pushed down on the stiff hat brim. His unruly brown hair pushed it right back up. "It looks like someone left a cheesebox on my head."

"A straw skimmer is just the thing for a young fellow," Indy's father, Professor Henry Jones, told him. "This is 1913, after all. Don't you want to look up-to-date?"

"But I had a perfectly fine hat. You know—the one that man gave me in Utah," Indy protested.

"That's fine for the country," Professor Jones said. "But we're in a big city now."

"Georgetown?" Indy glanced at the run-down buildings along the cobblestone street.

"Washington," the professor corrected his son. "I may be teaching at Georgetown University, but we are living in our nation's capital. And it's a very hot city in the springtime." He mopped his forehead with a handkerchief. "For this sort of weather, you need light—"

"—dumb-looking," Indy cut in.

"—clothes. Like that nice hat," Professor Jones finished. If he'd heard Indy, he didn't give any sign of it. Instead, he reached into his vest pocket and took out a gold watch. "I have a lecture to give in a few minutes. Do you want to come along, or can I leave you alone?"

"With this hat on, *everyone* will leave me alone." Indy sighed. "Go on, Dad. What trouble could I get into?"

"You always manage to surprise me." Henry Jones set off down the street. After a few steps, however, he turned back. "That

hat would look much better if you didn't just plunk it down on your head. Try a little style."

Tipping his own straw hat at a jaunty angle, the professor strolled off.

Still grumbling, Indy headed along the straggling, uneven street. Nobody was out. Everyone in Georgetown was avoiding the afternoon heat.

Indy looked at his reflection in an empty shop window. "A little style, huh?" He stepped into the doorway, using its plate glass as a mirror. First he tried tilting the hat on the back of his head. "Awful." Bringing the hat down forward made him look even worse. How about off to one side? "I look like I should be singing a song."

Then he caught a hint of movement in his makeshift mirror. Someone was moving behind him.

No, it was *three* people moving. A big, red-haired man had come up behind a young woman. He'd clapped a hand over her mouth. Another man, dark-haired with a beard, leapt from a horse-drawn carriage. Together, they struggled to take something from the girl. Obviously, the men hadn't seen Indy in the doorway. But they were going to see him now.

Indy dashed across the street. The two bruisers had their backs to him. The bearded one thrust his face close to the girl's, growling, "We've got you now, missy, and we'll have that book."

"You want to read? Read this!" Indy jumped onto the bearded man's back. Blackbeard stumbled to the ground, losing his grip on the young woman.

The girl took advantage of the rescue right away. As Blackbeard's hand left her arm, she aimed a kick at the bigger man's shin.

The redhead yelped, jumped back—and the girl was free. But before she'd run two steps, the man grabbed for her. Indy jumped in his way, only to be shoved aside.

Tottering back, Indy felt his hat fly off. That wasn't important. He had to stop this guy before his black-bearded pal got back into the fight.

Indy threw himself forward in a flying leap.

His arms wrapped around the redhead's legs in a football tackle. They both went down. But the hoodlum kicked free and started after the girl again.

Indy had lost his balance and his breath in the short tussle. When he got to his feet, the thug was out of reach. But the girl was halfway down the block, yelling her head off.

Then Indy heard a heel scrape on the slate sidewalk behind him. He jumped aside as a fist swished over his head. The bearded bruiser was back!

Indy had to dodge and dance as the man kept swinging. How could he get free to help the girl? But the girl was taking care of herself.

Windows overlooking the street clattered up as she shouted for help.

"Leave that girl alone!" someone yelled.

"Police! Police!" Several voices took up the cry.

The red-haired man stopped chasing the girl. He stared up at the dozens of witnesses glaring down at him. "What now, Beau?" he called to the black-bearded man.

"We get out of here."

The men crashed into Indy, bouncing him into a brick wall. They jumped into their carriage. Beau cracked the reins over the horses, and they sped off.

Indy pushed himself slowly off the wall. He was too late—the men had escaped. But at least the girl was safe. She came back, stopping in the middle of the street. Bending over, she picked something up, then headed back to Indy.

"I'm afraid this got run over," she said in a soft southern drawl. In her hand was his straw hat. The middle of it was crushed flat.

Indy couldn't help laughing. Maybe things were getting better.

He smiled as he looked up. Then he found himself staring. The girl was beautiful, about eighteen. A little more than four years older than Indy. She wore a broad-brimmed straw bonnet over golden-blond hair. Indy had seen statues of Greek goddesses that looked like her. Except this goddess had a sprinkle of freckles across her nose and cheeks. And her eyes were the bluest blue he'd ever seen.

"I'm glad you weren't gawping like that

when you jumped on those fellas," the girl told him. "We'd both be in trouble."

Indy realized two things. One, his face was turning bright red. Two, his mouth seemed to have gotten disconnected from his brain.

"It wasn't fair of me to say that," the girl apologized. "Not since you rescued me and all." She hesitated for a second, then stuck out her hand. "I'm Elizabeth Ravenall—Lizzie."

"I—I'm, uh, Henry Jones." He stopped. Had he really said Henry? "But people call me Indy—for Indiana."

Lizzie's eyebrows rose. "Sounds like a Yankee name to me."

"My dad and I have lived all over the country," Indy said. "You see, he's a professor. Right now, he's teaching at Georgetown University."

"The university?" Lizzie said excitedly. "I've come all the way from South Carolina to see a professor there. But I haven't been able to speak with him."

She looked hopefully at Indy. "Is your father a historian by any chance?"

Lost in those big blue eyes, Indy would

have given anything to say yes. But he had to shake his head. "Dad teaches Medieval Literature."

"Oh." Lizzie gave a little shrug. "Well, I guess you wouldn't know Dr. Walton then."

"You mean Dr. Zachary Walton?" A big smile spread across Indy's face.

"That's the very man," Lizzie said, amazed.

"He's a good friend of my father's." Indy felt his heart jump. He'd be able to help Lizzie, to keep on seeing her! "I'm sure Dad can get you two together. Should Dr. Walton know anything else? I—I mean, is there anything else I can do?"

Lizzie gave Indy a funny look. He realized he was babbling. "I want to show Dr. Walton my grandfather's secret journal," she said.

Indy ducked his head, trying to keep control of his mouth. "Is that all? I mean, I'm happy to do more."

Lizzie shook her head. "Just tell him it's about the years before the Civil War—and treasure."

Chapter 2

The next evening, the Jones family had two visitors at their boardinghouse.

The first was Lizzie Ravenall. When Professor Jones saw her coming up the stairs, he glanced at Indy with raised eyebrows. "My little boy is growing up."

"Come on, Dad." Indy could feel his cheeks growing warm. "She's just a girl."

Before he could say more, Lizzie had reached them. "Hi, Indy," she said, smiling.

"Uh, hello, Lizzie." Indy could feel himself turning shy. He'd fought bandits, faced lions and snakes, and nearly gotten killed. So why couldn't he talk normally when a pretty girl smiled at him? He took a deep breath. "Elizabeth Ravenall, this is my father, Professor Henry Jones."

Lizzie shook hands with Indy's dad. "Thank you for your help, sir."

"My pleasure, Miss Ravenall. Besides, Indy wouldn't give me any peace until I talked with Zachary," Professor Jones said. Indy could feel his ears turning red. But his father went on. "I thought we might talk here in our rooms, rather than the parlor. It's more private."

"I surely appreciate that, Professor." Lizzie clutched a package wrapped in brown paper to her chest. "I came a long way to see Dr. Walton. It took most of my money. But I think it will be worth it."

"Well, I think your determination is about to be rewarded," Indy's dad said. "I hear someone coming up."

Dr. Zachary Walton appeared a moment later. He was a tall man, but his shoulders were stooped, as if he'd spent most of his life at a desk. His hair was gray, and his long face always looked a little sad. But Dr. Walton's most noticeable feature was his mustache. It was large, gray, and carefully waxed into a handlebar shape.

Dr. Walton ran a finger over one side of his mustache. Then he bowed to Lizzie Ravenall. "So, you're the young lady who left so many messages at my office," he said. "Well, ma'am, why do you need to see this old Yankee?"

Lizzie waited until they were seated in Professor Jones's sitting room. Then she turned to Dr. Walton. "Sir, I know you're a great historian. You're the authority on the years before the War Between the States. Everyone's read your book, *The Storm Clouds Gather*. Even the folks back home in Carolina! We heard how you interviewed so many people—ex-senators, congressmen, plantation owners, even freed slaves. It's a wonder."

"I'm impressed that you know so much about my work," Walton said. "But I don't believe we've gotten to the reason for this meeting."

"That's a long story. It goes back fifty-five

years—to the days before the war," Lizzie told him. "But it may come down to the present day, as well."

"Tell away." Walton sat down with an interested expression on his face.

"It starts with my grandfather, Ashley Ravenall," Lizzie began. "Back in 1858, he was found dead, floating in a creek. Folks thought his horse had thrown him halfway across a bridge. But Grandfather was an excellent rider."

She shook her head and went on. "There's more to the mystery. Grandfather had been working on his will. He was riding to his lawyer to discuss it. Yet no papers were found on his body."

"Mysterious indeed," said Professor Jones.

"You mean suspicious," Indy said.

Lizzie shrugged. "It was both. Without a will, the estate dragged through the courts. The bank wound up owning Ravenall Hall and all the land."

"Your family lost everything?" Indy asked.

Lizzie nodded. "The overseer, Harlan Clegg, ran the place for the bank. After the war, he bought it for a song. Two of the three Ravenall boys died during the fighting. The third was my father. He went out west, to make a new family fortune." She blinked back tears. "It didn't work. He came home a sick man, married my mother, and died a couple of years after I was born. I—I hardly remember him."

"So you're the last of the Ravenalls?" said Dr. Walton.

"I am," Lizzie said. "And all I have left is the Ravenall name. It's Clegg County now. Harlan's son is the big gun there. He doesn't like Ravenalls." She tossed her head, sending her blond curls bouncing. "But then, we Ravenalls were never fond of him."

Dr. Walton looked up from his notebook. He'd been copying down everything Lizzie said. "I hope you don't mind my taking notes. It's the historian in me coming out. I've collected stories like these for years—volumes and volumes of journals."

He sighed and looked a bit older. "I have so little time left to capture the words of the people who lived before and during the war.

25

Many have passed on. Already we have legends where we should have truth."

"Well, it sounds as if your records will help keep things straight," Lizzie said.

"We should have a library devoted entirely to the Civil War era." Dr. Walton's eyes glowed as if he were preaching. Then the light dimmed a little. "That was why I came to Washington. I've talked to senators and congressmen. They all think the library is a fine idea. There's no money for it, but they think it's a fine idea." He sighed again. "That's *my* problem, not Miss Ravenall's. How does your story connect to the present day?"

"I found this." Lizzie unwrapped the paper from her parcel. Inside was a green leather book with tarnished gilt letters.

Indy squinted, trying to read the title. "*The Sermons of Cotton Mather*?"

"That's what it says. But look inside." She opened the book to show page after page of handwriting. "It's Grandfather's secret journal. It was hidden in the plantation library. My mother ended up with some of the books.

26

Harlan Clegg thought they weren't worth much."

Lizzie bit her lip, thinking back. "When Mama passed on, I decided to sell our things. I'd just finished secretarial school and was moving to Charleston to take a job. When I happened to open the book, I found this."

She showed the last entry to Dr. Walton. He read it aloud, while Indy and his father listened in fascination.

"So, your grandfather hid a treasure. But he never told his children how to find it," Walton said, tapping a finger on the page. "And it definitely says he was carrying his will into town."

"The important part, I think, is the mention of the kitchen slave—Harriet Robinson," Lizzie pointed out.

"I noticed that," Walton said. "Your grandfather must have been a mighty liberal man. In those days, most slaves had no last names."

"Grandfather wanted to be a good master. He even encouraged his people to take names."

"Have you spoken to this Harriet?" Walton asked. "Is she still alive?"

"I don't know," Lizzie admitted. "Harlan Clegg was a cruel master. Many slaves ran off. Most were brought back, dead or alive. Harriet Robinson was one of the lucky ones. She got clean away, probably because she had help."

"The Underground Railroad?" Professor Jones asked.

Lizzie nodded, and Dr. Walton smiled. "Now I begin to understand."

"I'm glad somebody does," Indy said. "What's this underground railroad? Sounds like they used a lot of tunnels."

"It wasn't exactly a railroad," Dr. Walton said. "There were no tracks or locomotives."

"Only some very brave, determined people," Indy's father went on. "The Underground Railroad helped slaves who escaped from plantations down south reach the North—where there was no slavery." He glanced over at Dr. Walton. "But then, this is Zachary's field of expertise."

"Back in those days, helping a slave escape was breaking the law," Dr. Walton explained. "It was stealing someone else's property. But people who hated slavery were willing to risk jail. They had secret rooms to hide escaped slaves. There were wagons with secret compartments, too. I've seen maps with hundreds of routes, going from town to town.

"There were houses where escapees could hide along the way. Stations, they were called. And the people who lived there were called stationmasters. Some people even went down south to lead slaves to freedom. They were known as conductors."

"And the whole thing was against the law?" Indy said.

"Down south, people were jailed for twelve years for helping runaways. The northern states weren't all that eager to return escaped slaves. But the federal government got in the act. Congress passed a Fugitive Slave Law. Then owners could come up north and drag their slaves home in chains. So the Underground Railroad extended its lines all the way to Canada. Slave-takers couldn't do their dirty work up there."

"It must have been quite an organization," Professor Jones said.

"It most certainly was. But there are a lot of unrecorded stories. That's why I try to talk to as many old-timers as possible. I need the facts." Walton sat a little straighter. "I'm one of the few people alive who know the exact escape routes."

"That's why I came to see you," Lizzie said. "I'd like to find which way Harriet went. It may tell me where she is now. If she's even still alive."

Zachary Walton shook his head. "You want to follow a fifty-year-old trail? All because of a vague mention of treasure in an old journal? It's hopeless."

"Not to everyone," Indy spoke up excitedly. "Lizzie, when those guys grabbed you, what did the one with the beard say? Something about a book—maybe the journal?"

Lizzie nodded, looking a little embarrassed. "I told you that Harlan Clegg's son—his name is Gideon—is the local king. Well, when I read the journal, I talked to some folks in Clegg County. I told them how it showed that old Harlan had stolen from Grandfather. Maybe I mentioned the treasure, too. . . . I guess Gideon must have heard. He made things mighty hot for me back home."

"Maybe Clegg's keeping up the heat," Indy suggested. "What if he sent those two strong-arms after you?"

They were all silent for a moment, taking that in. Then Zachary Walton slapped his hands down on his thighs so hard, everyone jumped. He had made his decision. "Miss Lizzie, I don't think it will be easy to find Harriet Robinson. And who knows if she can explain about this 'treasure.' "

Lizzie's face fell.

"But I'd be pleased to help you try and find your grandpa's treasure."

Lizzie Ravenall beamed at the gray-haired historian.

"I'd like to help, too." Indy blurted the words out before he knew it.

Professor Jones looked at his son in surprise. He was about to speak, but Indy talked fast. "You'll be busy at the university, Dad. And I bet they could use another pair of hands—or legs, or whatever."

"What they'll really need is luck," Professor Jones said slowly.

"Well, I can help find—"

"Son, I don't like to say this. But you tend to find only one thing."

"One thing?" Lizzie said.

"Trouble." Professor Jones shook his head. "In this case, Miss Ravenall, I think that's what you'll find anyway."

Chapter 3

Indy stifled a yawn the next morning. It was barely dawn, and he was standing outside the boardinghouse. The early-morning sun shone right into his eyes. He readjusted the old felt hat he'd gotten in Utah so the brim cut the glare.

Indy shifted impatiently from one foot to the other. He couldn't wait to begin the search for Harriet Robinson. Following the old escape routes would be exciting. And Dr. Walton had one of those new Ford motorcars! Adventure was just around the corner, and Indiana Jones was ready.

But instead of an engine, Indy heard the steady *clop-clop-clop* of horse's hoofs hitting the cobblestones. Was this when the milk wagons made their deliveries? Then an old black buggy pulled by two horses came into view. Sitting up on the driver's seat were Lizzie Ravenall and Zachary Walton.

"We'll be traveling over some mighty poor roads down in Virginia," Dr. Walton explained, jingling the reins. "So I thought it was best to ride in this old thing."

Disappointed, Indy jumped into the buggy. "I don't understand why we aren't checking in Washington first," he said. "Why go down to Virginia?"

"A lot of escape routes came together near Washington, but runaways avoided the city," Walton explained. "It was too easy to get caught crossing the bridges into town. The District of Columbia was a slave area, with lots of slave-catchers. There was a time when slaves were sold right in view of the Capitol."

Lizzie Ravenall shook her head. "Hard to believe."

"It was a strange time," Dr. Walton said. "Both North and South had strong feelings about slavery. Finally, they stopped arguing and started fighting—four years of civil war."

"Down south, we call it the War Between the States," Lizzie said.

"It was more than that," Walton added. "Whole families split when some members sided with the southern states—the Confederacy—while others stayed with the Union. Brother against brother. Friend against friend. I've heard the same sad story from many people. They tell how their best friend died in their arms—wearing the uniform of the other side."

Indy's eyes widened. "How could you fight your best friend?"

"It happened," Walton said sadly. "That's why my library is so important—it would help people understand."

The three fell silent as they passed through the quiet streets of Georgetown. Indy glanced shyly at Lizzie, who sat on Walton's far side. At least he wasn't babbling like an idiot today. Not yet, anyway.

They crossed a bridge over the Potomac River, heading south, then west. "We'll take the Leesburg to Georgetown Turnpike," Walton explained. "Then we'll check the south side of the Potomac. Overland escape routes could wander all over the place. But they all came together at river crossings. So we'll try Farmer's Crossing. It's the nearest Underground Railroad station. Runaways hid there till they could cross the river under cover of darkness."

They rattled along between green fields, with rolling hills in the distance. Lizzie didn't watch the countryside. Her eyes scanned the road ahead, eager to find the first stop on their search for Harriet Robinson—and treasure.

The station was a small, weather-beaten wooden farmhouse. The ruins of a barn stood behind it. "That could have been burned down in the war," Walton said. "There was a lot of fighting in this area. Hello!" he called, as he reined in the horses.

A gray-haired black man came out of the house. "You folks lost?"

"I'm looking for Mose Harker," Walton said.

The man leaned against a post on the porch. "Well, sir, you found him."

"I think we're probably looking for your father," Indy said. This man looked too young.

"You're a little late to meet him—or my mam." The man nodded over to a white rail fence by the side of the house. It surrounded two carefully tended headstones.

"Is it true they were stationmasters for the Underground Railroad?" Lizzie asked, sounding anxious.

Mose Harker nodded. "Mam and Pap, they were freeborn. Family's been free since 1813, when Judge Randolph let his people go. So, when some poor creature came on the run, trying for freedom, they'd help out. They told me stories about it."

"We're trying to trace a particular woman," Lizzie said. "Did you ever hear any stories about Harriet Robinson?"

Mose shook his head. "Don't think they ever mentioned names. Sorry." He thought for a second. "But I recollect hearing about another station by the river. It's some miles west of here."

"I know the place," Dr. Walton said. "We'll try there next."

"Thanks for your help," Indy added.

As the carriage started up again, Lizzie stared back at the graves. "They were brave folks. But I surely hope they didn't help Harriet Robinson."

Indy blinked.

"You mean we need live people if we're going to get solid facts." Dr. Walton nodded grimly. "Now you know how a historian feels."

Their next stop was another farmhouse. Larger and more prosperous, it was white-washed, with broad fields beyond. The young man chopping wood in the farmyard put down his ax when Walton questioned him. He wiped sweat off his pale freckled face. "That was back in my grandpappy's day. We didn't even live here then. I've heard stories that Crazy Hayward—that's what they called him—used to smuggle people through. But

. . ." The young man shrugged his shoulders.

Lizzie looked very gloomy as they clattered along the road. "We'll have to expect some setbacks along the way," Walton said gently. "But everyone won't have died or moved. Don't give up hope."

Their course took them through a range of hills. Watching the green Virginia countryside roll by, the historian suggested, "You know, it's possible Harriet didn't even pass through here. People escaped in all sorts of ways. One man packed himself in a crate and shipped himself to freedom. A couple escaped by having the wife disguise herself as a sickly white planter. She pretended to bring her husband along as a servant. Harriet might even have found a friendly ship's captain who let her sail north from Carolina."

"Are you saying we're wasting our time?" Lizzie asked, even more discouraged. "We'll never find her, or the treasure?"

"Well, we sure won't if we give up," Indy said. Their buggy reached the crest of a tall hill. At that moment, Indy suddenly rose in his seat, looking off behind them.

"I think we're being followed!" he said. "That wagon's been trailing along after us for a while. And they hang back whenever we stop to ask questions."

Dr. Walton looked worried. "Who could it be?"

"I don't want to find out on a lonely road." Indy quickly took the reins from Dr. Walton. He snapped them hard, and the horses broke into a gallop.

They raced downhill, toward a bend in the Potomac. "This will give us a good lead!" Indy shouted above the thud of horse's hoofs.

Dr. Walton tugged on his arm. "Stop! The station is right here!"

Indy reined in the buggy at the biggest farmhouse yet. It was built partly of stone, with whitewashed wooden walls.

"The people who own this farm are Quakers." Dr. Walton brushed off some dust from their wild ride and smoothed his mustache. "Their religion views fighting as a great evil and forbids it. Quaker teachings were also against slavery. Many Quakers worked on the Underground Railroad."

"Let's hope they can give us some help—and quickly," Lizzie said. "I don't like the idea of that wagon behind us."

They walked up to an elderly man sitting in a rocking chair on the porch. With his round pink face and big white beard, he looked like Santa Claus.

"We're looking for some information from before the war," Walton said.

"A great tragedy, the war," the man replied. "How can I help thee?"

"We understand you helped a number of slaves escape to the North," Lizzie said. "Was one of them a woman named Harriet Robinson?"

A slow smile spread across the old man's face. "Ah, Harriet. A brave young woman."

"She was here?" Lizzie said excitedly.

"Not only was she here but so was a slave-catcher. Thee knows, of course, that Quakers are not allowed to use force. In this case, Harriet herself saved the day."

"*She* took care of the slave-catcher?" Indy said.

41

"In the Bible, Samson used the jawbone of an ass to smite his enemies." The elderly Quaker laughed. "Harriet used a large cast-iron skillet."

"A frying pan?" Indy couldn't believe it!

"She brought it from where she'd been a servant—down in the Carolinas, I believe." The old man's face was a mass of wrinkles as he smiled at the memory. "The slave-taker nearly caught her as she came out of the woods. But she struck him and made good her escape."

"I wish we had her here now," Indy interrupted.

"Don't we all," said Lizzie.

"I meant, in case there's a fight." Indy was staring grimly up the road.

Coming down the hillside was a large wagon. Two of the four men riding in it looked familiar. Unpleasantly familiar.

One was big, beefy, and red-haired. The other was shorter, with dark hair and a beard. Indy remembered them both.

They were the men who'd attacked Lizzie Ravenall.

Chapter 4

Indy looked around at empty fields. There wasn't another house in sight. They had nowhere to run. Turning to the old Quaker, he said, "Those men in the wagon are after us. Can you help?"

"This is a peaceful house," the man said. "There are no weapons inside."

He thought for a second, biting his lip. "But I may have a way to escape."

"How?" Indy asked.

"Back before the war, our neighbors knew we helped runaways," the man said. "They watched the house, hoping to catch the slaves when they left." He smiled. "We needed a way out that they couldn't see."

Moving briskly, the Quaker took Dr. Walton and Lizzie by the arm. "Come."

He rushed them into the house, leading everyone into the parlor. The snug room had wooden paneling and a huge fireplace.

The elderly man stepped up to a large wooden panel. "Here it is," he said, pushing at one corner. Nothing happened.

"It won't budge!" The man turned to Indy. "Son, give this thing a push."

Indy put his hand where the old man's had been, and shoved. The panel still didn't move. "Put thy shoulder into it," the old man said.

"Please, Indy," Lizzie added nervously.

That was all Indy needed to hear. Throwing all his weight against the panel, he pushed as hard as he could. With a loud creak the panel suddenly swung around. Indy nearly went tumbling down a staircase that led into darkness.

"Our old escape tunnel," the man said proudly. "I dug it myself." He stepped over to the mantel and came back with three candles. "It leads to the boathouse by the river. I still keep a rowboat there for fishing. Row upstream, till—"

"Until we come to the Gillis house on the Maryland side," Dr. Walton finished for him. "I know the route."

The helpful Quaker nodded. "Just be careful in the tunnel. No one's used it for near on fifty years."

Lizzie and Dr. Walton lit their candles and stepped through the secret panel. Outside, they heard the jingle of harness as their pursuers' wagon drew up. "Hey, in the house!" a man's voice called out.

"In you go, boy," the old Quaker told Indy. "Now give me a hand from your side. Help me push this panel back."

Indy heaved. The wood clunked into place, but the movement blew out his candle. "Perfect," Indy muttered as he turned around in complete darkness. "Lizzie?" he called hopefully. "Dr. Walton?"

They'd both gone ahead. Indy had to grope his way down the rough-cut stone steps. One step wasn't where he expected it. Indy slid the rest of the way down on the seat of his pants. "*Really* perfect," he groaned, landing on a dirt floor. "All I need now is some snakes."

Indy stood up carefully and touched a dirt wall. With one hand on the cool earth, he set off toward a dim glow. Inching along the passageway, bit by bit, Indy couldn't help imagining all sorts of creepy-crawly things in the darkness. At last—Lizzie and Dr. Walton!

Lizzie gave a little yip of surprise when Indy loomed out of the darkness.

"What happened to your candle?" she asked, pulling a cobweb out of her hair.

"It blew out when I shut the panel," Indy explained.

Lizzie flicked the cobweb off her fingers. "This treasure hunting is dirty work," she said, making a face.

Indy looked at the ceiling, only inches above their heads. "It could be dangerous, too. Look how this is sagging. In fact—"

A huge clump of dirt fell on his head. Dr.

Walton gasped. Indy tore off his hat to give it a shake. That just spread more dirt around.

"Hey, watch that!" Lizzie said.

"No—move it!" Indy took her hand, and used her candle to light his. He led them along, moving as fast as he could without putting out the flame. Maybe it was because they were disturbing the tunnel. Or maybe it was due to its age. But more and more dirt began dribbling down on them.

A mini-landslide suddenly roared down. It knocked Dr. Walton to the floor. His candle dropped and went out. Lizzie and Indy each grabbed one of the old man's arms, helping him up. As they hurried along, they stumbled through a growing rain of dirt. Just as they reached a stone-lined room, they heard a muffled rumble behind them. Then came a cloud of dust. Lizzie's candle blew out.

"Looks like we brought the house down," Indy said with a grin.

"Indy! We could have been killed!" Dr. Walton's voice was shaky.

"Look on the bright side. At least, those guys can't follow us!" Indy raised his candle so its circle of light showed another staircase. "Hey—here's the way out."

A few moments later, they were pushing against another secret panel, which opened into the boathouse. The place was empty except for an old rowboat.

"I sure hope this boat holds up better than the tunnel," Indy said.

Hidden by trees, they carried the boat down to the riverbank. Indy looked back at the farmhouse. Were Beau and his friends still there?

He held the rowboat steady as Lizzie and Dr. Walton climbed aboard. Then he took the oars and started to row. Beyond the boathouse, they could hear shouting. The thugs were searching the farm—but couldn't find them.

Leaning into each stroke, Indy took them across to the far side. Then he rowed upstream until the old Quaker farm was out of sight.

Lizzie rowed for a while, then Dr. Walton. "We'll have a walk ahead of us," Walton said as he finally brought them to the Maryland shore.

"Too bad we couldn't have fit the buggy onto the boat." Indy waded through the shallows, pulling the boat closer to dry land.

He held it as Dr. Walton climbed out. Then he took Lizzie by the waist and swung her onto the riverbank.

Indy had never been so close to her before. He didn't pay attention to his footing and slipped on a rock. Lizzie landed safely on shore. Indy wound up sitting in water—up to his neck. Even in cold water his cheeks were burning.

"Indy, stop fooling around," said Dr. Walton. "We still have to find Harriet."

The three walked inland and soon found a road. About a half-mile along, a farm wagon rattled up behind them. A single plodding horse pulled it, and the driver seemed asleep on his seat. Indy flagged him down and begged for a ride for the three of them.

The wagon didn't move fast. But it was easier than walking to the Gillis farm.

The farmhouse was a two-story stone building, surrounded by green fields. Old Man Gillis was leaning on the front gate, enjoying the view.

The farmer was old, but his seamed face was a healthy bronze from working in the sun. A pair of sharp blue eyes watched closely as the visitors pulled up.

When Lizzie Ravenall asked him about Harriet Robinson, the old man smiled. "I remember—the girl with the big skillet. You know, she cooked dinner for us. Mighty handy with that pan."

"In more ways than one," Indy said. "She used it on a slave-taker back in Virginia."

Mr. Gillis nodded and laughed. "I heard that story. She just stayed with us overnight, then headed north."

"Do you have any idea where she might have gone?" Lizzie asked.

"Christiana, up in Pennsylvania," Gillis said. "I guess I suggested it. It's a town where a group of Negro freemen settled."

"Christiana, eh?" Walton frowned, thinking of the possible routes.

"Thanks, sir," Lizzie said to the old farmer.

But Mr. Gillis wasn't looking in her direction. He scanned the area beyond the road. "Somebody's moving through that field," he said.

Indy whipped around to the grainfield behind them. Gillis's eyes were sharp indeed. There was a barely noticeable path of shaking grain stalks—heading straight for them.

Two men burst from the field. They were big and burly, dressed in rough clothes. Indy didn't recognize either of them. But the strong-arms recognized Lizzie.

"There she is!" one of them shouted.

Indy grabbed the girl's arm. "Run for it!"

Dr. Walton and Mr. Gillis moved to block the gate as Indy and Lizzie ran across the farmyard. But Indy knew that an elderly man and a historian past his prime would hardly slow down those two gorillas. In the distance, he heard the clatter of a wagon charging up the road.

A quick glance over his shoulder showed Indy all he wanted to know. Standing in the wagon, gripping the reins, was the black-bearded man—Beau. "Come *on!*" Indy shouted to Lizzie.

Together they dashed across the porch and into the farmhouse.

"Chester!" Indy heard a woman's voice call

51

from the rear of the house. "What's all the hoo-rah outside?"

Indy looked around wildly. There was a broom closet off the hallway to the kitchen. Indy yanked open the closet door and hustled Lizzie inside.

He got the door closed just as footsteps sounded in the hallway. They stood together in the darkness, still breathing hard from their run. Where were the footsteps going? Lizzie grabbed his arm, startling him. Indy nearly went through the ceiling. "Don't do that!" he whispered.

The footsteps moved away. Indy didn't know if that was a good sign or not. Maybe jumping into the closet had been a bad move. They had no place to go. Should he open the closet door now? No, he and Lizzie might step right into the arms of the men they were trying to escape.

A woman's shouting voice came from outside. "What do you jaspers think you're up to?"

Then came the crash of a shotgun going off.

Standing in the dark, Lizzie gave a little cry. Her fingers dug into Indy's arm. "What's going on?" she whispered.

Indy had no answer. But from the sound of things, the wagon was now moving away—fast!

Indy eased the closet door open. He pried Lizzie's fingers off his arm and stepped out. Right onto a large, creaking floorboard.

Then Indy heard a metallic *click*. He froze. In front of him was an elderly woman—with a double-barreled shotgun in her hands.

Those two black holes looked as large as anything he'd ever seen in his life. Indy stared at them, almost hypnotized. He hardly heard what the woman was saying. She finally had to shout.

"I asked what you're doing in my house, you ruffian!" The woman's knuckles were white from gripping the shotgun's stock.

"If you don't answer in three seconds, you'll get a lot worse than your friends outside!"

Chapter 5

"Martha! Martha! What are you doing?"

Mr. Gillis came through the door, a look of horror on his face.

Indy dropped to the floor, afraid that the gun in the woman's hand would go off.

There was no blast. Indy looked up to see the woman holding on to Mr. Gillis. "Oh, Chester! I saw you lying by the gate. Those jayhawkers were standing over you . . ."

"Thank heaven you brought out that old scattergun," Mr. Gillis said. "It scared them off. But not before they took your friend, young man."

"Took?" Indy shot to his feet.

"They grabbed him and dragged him into their wagon," Mr. Gillis explained. "Then they headed back down the road."

He looked around. "Where's the young lady who was with you?"

Lizzie stepped out of the closet.

Mrs. Gillis (as Indy figured she must be) almost brought up the shotgun again. "Another one!" she exclaimed. "Chester, will you please tell me what's going on here."

"These folks came to ask about a runaway we helped years ago. Remember Harriet Robinson?"

Mrs. Gillis had to smile. "The one with the skillet?"

Indy didn't smile. "We've got to follow those kidnapers."

"Take time to get the wagon." Mr. Gillis said.

Indy had a different idea.

Moments later, he and Lizzie were riding double on a horse. With only a blanket for a saddle, Lizzie clung tightly to Indy as they bounced along.

"We've got to save poor Dr. Walton!" Lizzie

kicked her heels into the horse's flanks. "I got him into this."

Even carrying two passengers, the horse made better time than the kidnapers' heavily loaded wagon. By the time Indy and Lizzie reached the hillcrest, they could see the escaping wagon. It was halfway back to the river.

"There they are!" Lizzie cried. "Let's catch up! Come on, horse, come on!" She kicked her heels again, urging their mount to greater speed.

But Indy hauled back on the reins. The confused horse lurched forward, then stumbled back. Their blanket-saddle was slipping dangerously as Indy yelled, "Cut that out, Lizzie! We don't want to catch up with them."

Lizzie stopped kicking, nearly falling off the horse. "We don't? You are the most contrary— Why are we chasing them, then?"

"We want to see where they're taking Dr. Walton. But we don't want those strong-arms to see us."

Indy couldn't see Lizzie's expression, but he could tell she was puzzled.

"Look, Lizzie, there are four guys on that wagon," he explained. "I see only two of us."

"So then, what can we do?"

"Once we know where they're keeping Dr. Walton, we wait for dark. *Then* we rescue him."

"I guess that makes sense," Lizzie finally said. She patted the side of the horse. "Okay, boy, don't lose them."

They rode for the rest of the day, back across the Potomac into Virginia. But the kidnapers didn't head for Washington. They were still deep in the country when they finally stopped the wagon.

Lizzie and Indy almost rode past the hideout. Only the glow of oil lamps in an old, ruined barn stopped them.

"I wonder if this barn got wrecked in the war," Indy said. He guided the horse to a little patch of woods.

Lizzie peered at the barn through the branches of a bush. "How are we going to get in there without being seen?"

"That's just half the problem," Indy told her. "We also have to get out."

Lizzie looked at him in the growing dusk. "I hope you have a plan."

"Actually, I do." Indy grinned as he opened the coil of rope he'd carried on his shoulder. Using his pocketknife, he cut off several pieces and began knotting them together. "It sounds like the horses are in that little field behind the barn." In the distance, they could hear the animals nickering.

Indy handed Lizzie two improvised sets of reins. "You've got to get these ropes onto the horses. Then lead them back here, among the trees. With this one here, we'll each have a horse to escape on."

"Do you think Dr. Walton can ride?" Lizzie asked.

"It's funny what you can do when a gang of crooks is chasing you," Indy told her. "Just do your part."

Lizzie hefted the ropes. "And what will you be doing?"

Indy shrugged. "I'll be in the barn, getting Dr. Walton out."

They crept together through the tall grass.

Weeds kept tickling Indy's nose. This is no time to sneeze, he told himself. At last, they reached the clearing by the barn. "This is where we part company," Indy said. "You head off for the horses. I'll see how I can get inside."

He snaked his way along the ground until he reached the barn. Some of the boards had rotted, and all of them were warped. Huge chinks gaped between them. Indy had his choice of peepholes.

Peering into the barn, Indy couldn't believe his luck. He was looking right into an old stall. But now it had been pressed into service as a jail. Zachary Walton sat on a bale of hay, his face in his hands. Beyond him, in the main part of the barn, the thugs had set up an old crate. In its center sat an oil lamp. The strong-arm types sat around it, playing poker. Indy could see three of them, looking at their cards.

A plan immediately formed in Indy's mind. First he'd distract the men. Then he'd get in, rescue Dr. Walton, and cover their escape. All he needed was a decent rock . . .

After scrabbling around in the barnyard

dirt, Indy came up with a pair of good-sized stones. He crept around to the front of the barn. One door hung off its hinges. That gave him a fair look—and shot—into the building.

Indy had eyes only for the lamp. Hit that, and the barn would be plunged into darkness. The guards wouldn't know what hit them. Indy wound up for his best fastball.

"I wouldn't do that if I were you, boy."

The voice came from behind Indy. He whirled around, ready for a fight. Instead, he let the stones fall from his hands.

The man who'd gotten the drop on him was his old enemy, black-bearded Beau. And there was someone else with him. One of his hands held Lizzie Ravenall firmly by the arm. The other was clamped over her mouth.

"Good—no rocks," Beau said. "Now, go on in."

Within minutes, Indy found himself with each wrist tied to a stall slat.

"Oh, Indy! Why did you come after me?" Dr. Walton cried, as he was brought out to sit on another hay bale, beside Lizzie.

"Mighty lucky I decided to go out for a

walk," Beau said. "Now, Miss Lizzie, let's get down to business. My employer wants a book you have."

"You mean Gideon Clegg," Lizzie said angrily. "Well, I don't have it. I left it in a safe place. He won't get his hands on it." Lizzie had no intention of telling the men she'd left the journal with Professor Jones.

"What do we do now, Beau?" one man asked.

"We make Miss Lizzie want to get that book for us."

The thug shifted uneasily. "I never beat on a woman before."

"I don't think we need to do that," Beau said. "We've got two of Miss Lizzie's friends here. Suppose we make their lives miserable? Then she'll tell us where that book is at. Who'll be first?"

He took a moment to examine Dr. Walton, then shook his head. "Too old to stand up to much wear and tear. We'll go with the Yankee brat. See how much punishment he can take. Besides, I think Miss Lizzie is a bit sweet on him."

"Why do you think—" Lizzie's voice choked

off in horror. Beau's redheaded assistant came back from the wagon carrying a bull-whip. "You can't mean to—"

"I surely can, missy," Beau told her, as he took the whip. "Ever seen what ten feet of Carolina blacksnake can do, boy?"

With an easy flick he sent the whip un-coiling. The tip smashed into the stall rail inches from Indy's bound wrist, with a deaf-ening crack. The wood splintered.

Beau snapped the whip again to whisk away Indy's hat. Then he played a game of "how close can you go?" all around Indy's face. The tip nearly touched Indy several times. He felt a breeze each time the whip cracked.

"Stop it! Stop it!" Lizzie screamed.

"Well, now, I'd like to. But you haven't told me what I want to know yet," Beau told her. The whip cracked barely an inch from In-dy's chin. "But I surely hope you tell me soon."

He flicked the whip past Indy's ear. "All this work makes a man's arm tired. Sooner or later, I'm gonna make a mistake!"

Chapter 6

The mistake that happened wasn't exactly what Beau had in mind. While he'd been trying to scare Lizzie, Indy had been busy.

He rubbed the ropes on his right hand against the section of rail Beau had splintered. One by one, he felt the fibers in the rope break apart against the jagged wood. Indy flinched as the whip snaked toward his face again. But he forced his eyes to stay open.

"All right, I'll talk," Lizzie yelled, as Beau

snapped the whip again. "I'll tell you where the blamed book is!"

Beau pulled back on the whip, slowing it. The tip seemed to float toward Indy's face.

This was Indy's one chance. He wrenched his arm against the weakened cord that bound it. The rope broke. His hand flew free.

Indy stared hard at the end of the black-snake whip. It seemed to move in slow motion. He grabbed for the tip of the whip— and got hold. One jerk, and the whip handle suddenly sailed out of Beau's grasp. It swept back toward Indy, who managed to catch it one-handed.

Before anyone could stop her, Lizzie ran to Indy's side. She tore at the rope binding his other wrist.

Beau took a step toward Lizzie. The whip snapped just in front of his nose.

"Don't you move," Indy warned. "Don't you move a muscle. I've got a real bad temper. You never know when I might lash out."

The three men around the crate table rose to their feet. Indy cracked the whip at Beau again.

"Tell them to sit down, and keep very still, if they like your face the way it is," Indy growled.

Beau nervously licked his lips and told his men to keep their places. "Look, son, don't get carried away." The head strong-arm glanced anxiously at the long, black whip.

Indy moved suddenly, and Beau flinched. But the whip didn't crack—Indy just picked up his hat. "You can't hope to get out. There's four of us between you and the door," the thug said.

"What if I do—*this*!" The whip lashed out again and caught the base of the oil lamp. The lantern toppled over, leaving the barn in sudden darkness.

"What the—" one thug yelled.

"Hey!"

"Where'd they go?"

Indy and Lizzie dashed for the door, dragging Dr. Walton with them.

The redhead blundered into the crate table, knocking it over. Oil from the lamp spilled over the hay on the floor. There must have been an ember glowing on the lamp wick, because tongues of flame suddenly erupted inside the old barn.

With wild yells one man rolled around on the floor, trying to put out a fire on his pants. Another flapped an old horse blanket, in an attempt to smother the flames.

"Forget that!" Beau yelled. "They're getting away."

Indy burst through the barn doors. But he didn't run for the woods. He led his two friends around the side of the barn.

"Can't—make—" Dr. Walton puffed as Indy vaulted over a rail fence.

As Indy had hoped, Lizzie had put the rope reins on the horses before Beau caught her. Now Indy managed to get hold of the trailing ropes and brought the frightened horses to the fence.

Lizzie had the gate open. Zachary Walton scrambled onto the back of one horse. Lizzie climbed aboard the other as Indy rounded up the one he and Lizzie had ridden. They charged down a road barely visible in the moonlit night. Behind them Gideon Clegg's bruisers stumbled out of the barn.

"It will probably burn to the ground," Lizzie said, glancing over her shoulder. Flames were licking the whole building.

"Who cares?" Indy coaxed his horse into a gallop. Well behind them now, Beau and his people shouted useless threats.

"Let's stop a moment," panted Dr. Walton. "We must plan our next step." Even in a wild escape Dr. Walton managed to sound like a teacher preparing his next lesson. They brought the horses to a stop. "Perhaps we should take a train to Christiana, from Washington. That's where Mr. Gillis thought Harriet was going."

"Maybe she's still there," Lizzie said hopefully. "Pennsylvania was a free state."

"Yes, but it was mighty close to slave territory," Dr. Walton pointed out. "Most runaways were afraid of slave-hunters. They usually moved much farther north. Christiana was too hot for ex-slaves—and Washington will be too hot for us. What if Clegg's men come looking for us? I think we should pack our bags and head for Union Station."

Indy liked the plan. "We'll ride the Aboveground Railroad," he said, "at least as far as Philadelphia."

They caught the first train out of Washington. It was a local that leisurely chugged its way across Maryland into Delaware.

Lizzie stared at the scenery slowly passing in the window. "It will take us forever to get to Christiana at this rate," she complained. "I think we should have waited for an express."

Dr. Walton was on his feet, smoothing his mustache and pacing around the train compartment. "I wouldn't want to be at the station if Beau and his people came along." He gave a little shudder.

"Relax, Doctor," Indy said with a grin. "We've lost them. I bet we were out of town before they even made it in. Remember, they had to walk all the way."

"Unless they hitched a ride," Walton muttered gloomily. He continued pacing. As they pulled into a small station, he walked to the door. "Excuse me," he said. "I think I'll get a bit of air on the depot platform."

"He seems powerfully nervous," Lizzie said.

"Come on, Lizzie. He's been chased, captured, and rescued. And he's a bit old for all this running around."

While they waited at the station, an express train roared by.

"If I had the money, I would always travel express." Lizzie watched the cars whiz past.

They sat for long minutes in silence. Lizzie stared out the window, and Indy stared at Lizzie. When things got exciting, he'd forget how pretty she was. But now . . .

She's really some girl, he thought. We barely have a clue about Harriet and the treasure. But she won't give up. We could go on together—

But they *wouldn't* go on. This adventure would end. If it turned out well, Lizzie would be a rich young heiress. And he was only a kid—a professor's son. If they weren't successful . . . Indy shifted uncomfortably. It seemed disloyal to hope that Lizzie wouldn't find her fortune.

"Indy?"

He blinked and turned to Lizzie.

"You had just the funniest expression on your face. What were you thinking?"

"Thinking?" Indy said. "Oh, I was just, um, wondering. If you find this treasure, what will you do with it?"

Lizzie sighed. "When I was a little girl, I dreamed of suddenly becoming rich. I'd buy back Ravenall Hall, get lovely gowns for Mama, and throw glorious parties. The Cleggs would be so embarrassed, they'd leave the county."

"And now?"

"Mama's gone, and it looks as if Gideon Clegg will rule Clegg County forever." Lizzie shrugged. "There's nothing to keep me in Carolina. If I had money, I could leave. Go somewhere and get a real education. Maybe a university, like Georgetown."

She glanced at Indy. "It would be nice to go where I had a friend."

A friend! Indy thought. She thinks I'm a friend. The idea of being in the same town with Lizzie warmed his heart—until he remembered his father. Dad would probably move on to some other teaching post. Indy wondered if Professor Jones could be persuaded to leave him behind.

Indy entertained himself with thoughts of Lizzie and Georgetown until Dr. Walton came back in. A moment later, the train lurched forward again.

The local train rattled on for about an hour, making three more stops. They'd just left Wilmington when Indy's stomach began to rumble. He had to have a snack. "I'm going to look for the dining car," he announced, getting to his feet. "Anyone want to come?"

Dr. Walton shook his head. He was busy making notes for his Civil War library. And Lizzie, still sitting by the window, had fallen asleep.

Indy walked toward the rear of the train, whistling to himself. After all the running around, it was a relief to be alone.

He found the dining car, with its shining white tablecloths and glittering silverware. The waiter led him through the nearly empty car. They passed a table where a man sat alone. He'd just finished his coffee and was dabbing his mouth with a big white napkin. The napkin came down just as Indy walked by.

Both Indy and the man froze in surprise. The waiter had blocked the man's view of Indy.

And, until the last moment, that napkin had blocked Indy's view of Beau.

Chapter 7

Indy tapped the waiter's shoulder. "I won't be sitting after all," he said.

Behind him Beau tossed some bills on the table and rose from his seat.

What now? Indy wondered. Beau had just cut off his retreat. And anyway, did he want to lead this thug back to Dr. Walton and Lizzie?

Indy continued on through the dining car, toward the rear of the train. He thought feverishly. How many more cars were there? No need to look back and check if he was being followed. Indy caught Beau's reflection in the glass on the door as he changed cars.

Picking up his pace, Indy moved into the next car. Beau continued pursuing him. Indy hurried to keep his small lead. The question was, what could he do with it? He was moving through a regular passenger coach. Dozens of people sat on the big leather seats. Should he stop where he was? Call for a conductor?

He turned in the middle of the aisle, ready to face Beau. Then he saw that the black-bearded man had one hand in his jacket pocket.

Beau had a gun! If Indy tried for a showdown, there'd be shooting. He whipped back around and rushed down the aisle. How could he expose a coach full of people to gunplay?

Then an even colder thought hit him. What was he going to do when he ran out of cars? He'd be alone then—just him, and Beau, and the gun. Indy broke into a trot, frantically scanning the coach. No place to hide.

Two cars later, there was nowhere to run. Indy faced the blank wall of a boxcar. There was no connecting door!

This is it, Indy thought. The end of the line. Then he noticed a metal ladder set into the wood. He could climb to the roof.

Indy leapt for the ladder and scrambled up. From the top of the boxcar he jumped to the roof of the coach he'd just left. If he didn't make too much noise, he had a chance to surprise Beau.

Below him Indy heard the carriage door slam open. For a moment there was silence. Then came a low, evil chuckle. Beau must think he's got me now, Indy thought.

He braced himself, waiting. Soon he saw Beau's back as the thug climbed clumsily up the ladder. His right hand wasn't in his pocket anymore. It held a pearl-handled revolver.

Beau kept the gun aimed at the boxcar roof as he slowly rose to the top of the ladder. He never expected Indy to come at him from behind.

Indy's foot landed perfectly, smacking into

the wrist of Beau's gun hand. The revolver flew through the air. It landed on the gravel by the train tracks below.

Beau nearly landed there, too. He grabbed desperately at the metal ladder as Indy righted himself on the roof of the passenger car.

Indy sprinted along the roof of the carriage. The train was moving at a pretty fast clip. Wind tugged at his clothes, keeping him crouched down.

What should he do now? He'd gotten rid of Beau's gun, but that was only half the problem. He was still alone with Beau on top of the train. If the big man caught up with him . . .

Indy heard a thump from behind. He turned. Beau had made it to the top of the car. "Boy," the thug yelled, "you keep making a pest of yourself. I'm gonna have to take care of you."

Beau lurched after Indy, who had now reached the far end of the carriage. Indy didn't hang around to meet the angry thug. He took a running start and jumped the four-foot gap to the roof of the next car.

Indy dashed from car to car. Just staying on his feet was a battle as the train swayed from side to side. Then the train slowed down, taking a curve around a hill. When Indy saw what was ahead, he got an idea.

"Ha, Beau! You'll never catch me!" he yelled back to the thug. He began running for all he was worth. He had to keep Beau's attention on him, not on what was coming up.

Indy raced along the top of a passenger coach. Judging from the food smells wafting up, the next car was the dining car. He jumped for its roof. Behind him he heard Beau pounding along.

"I'll get you, you little—"

Beau's voice broke off, and Indy knew why. He'd finally noticed what Indy had already seen. There was a footbridge over the railroad tracks, and it was coming up on them right now. The bridge was too low to let them stand. Beau dove for the roof of the carriage.

But Indy had reached the end of the dining car. He swung down, to land on the platform between carriages. As he ran through the next coach, he felt the train coming to a halt. That was no surprise. Where there were footbridges, there were usually stations.

At last, Indy was back where he'd started. He burst into the compartment to find the scene almost unchanged. Zachary Walton was still writing in his notebook. Lizzie was still asleep.

Indy grabbed their bags off the overhead racks. "We've got to get off here!" he said, shaking Lizzie awake.

"What—why?" Lizzie managed.

"Beau's on the train, and he's only seconds behind me. We've got to lose him."

"How do you intend to do that?" Dr. Walton asked.

"We wait till the very last moment. Then, just as the train is starting up, we jump off."

Walton looked doubtful. But Indy herded the historian and the girl along, like a sheepdog moving a flock. The train had stopped now, and he could hear the conductor yelling, " 'Board!"

"Now!"

They ran for the end of the car. Dr. Walton

jumped off just as the train jerked into motion. He stumbled on the station platform
but stayed on his feet. Lizzie made a grace-
ful landing. Indy tossed out the bags, then
jumped himself. The train was really moving by then. He landed hard, hitting the
platform at knee, hip, and shoulder.

Lizzie dashed over. "Are you all right?"
She threw an arm around Indy as he shakily
pushed himself up.

"Did Beau or anyone else get off?"

Lizzie scanned the station platform. "No."

"Then I'm fine. Better than fine. Just a few
bruises."

"But what do we do now?" Walton wanted
to know.

"Let's see if we can hire a carriage," Lizzie
said. "We still have to get to Christiana."

"You young folk take care of it." Walton
headed for the depot building. "I just want
to sit down." The doctor moved a little stiffly,
Indy noticed. Maybe he hadn't made as good
a landing as it seemed.

The town livery stable had a buggy for
rent. Indy and Lizzie picked up Dr. Walton,

then headed west and north into Pennsylvania. Indy kept an eye on their rear all the way.

At last, they reached Christiana. Some kind of fair was going on, and the streets of the small town were packed. People milled around, looking at the gaily decorated booths. There were games of skill and chance. Normally, Indy would have stopped to play. But they had a bigger game to win—a real treasure hunt.

They had their usual problems getting answers. Some people were dead, others had moved. And some people were just fine, but wandering through the fair.

At one booth they found a grandfatherly black man who remembered the girl with the skillet. He gave them the next stop on Harriet's route. As they climbed back into their buggy, Indy had a bad moment. Looking out over the crowd, he caught a glimpse of a man with a black beard.

Lizzie saw the look on his face. "Indy! What's wrong?"

"I think I just saw Beau."

Lizzie gave his shoulder a shove. "Oh, come on. He lost us back at that train station. How would he be able to find us now?"

Dr. Walton carefully smoothed one side of his handlebar mustache. "A lot of the farmers hereabouts still wear beards, son. 'Whiskers like hay,' we city folk call it. One black beard does not a villain make."

They had excellent luck across Pennsylvania and into upstate New York. Lots of old-timers still lived there, and many told stories of a girl with a skillet. People actually remembered Harriet—maybe this hunt would work out after all!

Only two things dampened Indy's mood. First, he was worried for Dr. Walton. The old man always seemed tired. He walked slowly, and more and more, he'd give the "young folk" an address to check while he sat for a while.

The second thing worried Indy even more. Several times along the way, he thought they were being followed. He didn't mention it— having Lizzie laugh at him once was bad enough.

After two weeks' search, the trail finally led them to Massachusetts and into the city of Boston.

Lizzie shivered in the brisk New England breeze. "I hope we're getting close." She hugged herself for warmth. "This Yankee weather makes me downright homesick."

Walking along a red-brick street, Dr. Walton checked the piece of paper in his hand. "We must be near."

Indy pointed at a steeple rising on the next block. "That should be the Arbor Street Church. Now let's see if we can find that antislavery preacher you told us about."

The pastor's house was around the corner. It was a cozy two-story building. Lizzie eagerly ran up the stairs to the bellpull.

A pale, gray-haired, heavyset woman answered the door. She held a feather duster in her hand and gave them an annoyed look.

"We'd like to see the Reverend Porter, please," Lizzie said.

The woman shook her head. "Reverend Porter passed away long ago! It must have been around 1867."

Lizzie stared in shock. But she wasn't about to give up. Not after spending weeks and coming hundreds of miles on this hunt. "Is there anyone else here from the days before the war? We're trying to trace a runaway—"

She didn't get any further. The woman began to close the door. "I'm sorry, young lady, but that was more than fifty years ago."

Lizzie turned in desperation to Dr. Walton. He shook his head sadly. "Boston's a big city. It was full of antislavery activists—and the Reverend Porter knew them all. He could have sent Harriet on to any of them. I'm afraid the chain breaks here, Lizzie. We won't find Harriet. There were five routes out of Boston, in all directions."

Hanging her head, Lizzie sighed. "We knew this could happen. But to come so far . . ."

They headed back to the hotel where they were staying. Walton spoke up. "Since we're in Boston, I'd like to arrange an appointment for tomorrow to talk with Garrick Lloyd. He was a very important leader of the antislavery movement. When my library is established, it should include an interview with him "

Indy had to smile at the historian's confidence. One project had failed, but he moved right on to the next. And how sure he was that his library would be built!

"I surely think an interview will make a fine addition," Lizzie said. "And since you're here in Boston, you should make the most of it." Even though she'd failed to find the treasure, Lizzie tried to sound cheerful. It almost broke Indy's heart.

"Do you need someone to take dictation?" Lizzie went on with a grin. "I've been trained as a secretary, after all. May as well get some practice in before I go home to work."

In the end, they all went to visit Garrick Lloyd. The old man's small parlor was crowded with furniture. Lloyd sat in an overstuffed chair, a blanket wrapped around him. His skin seemed as thin and brittle as parchment. It was stretched tight over a bald head with little wisps of white hair over the ears. But the man's deep-set eyes still glittered with spirit and interest.

"You edited *The Voice of Freedom* from the 1840s, right through the crisis, and into the war," Dr. Walton began. "What is your greatest memory of those days?"

For the next two hours Indy listened in fascination as Garrick Lloyd remembered battles, struggles, and decisions from fifty years ago. After an hour, a nurse came in, but Lloyd waved the woman away.

Finally, the old man leaned back in his chair. "So, Doctor, what brings you up to these parts?"

Garrick Lloyd's face lit up as he heard the story of the Ravenall treasure and the woman they'd been searching for.

"Harriet Robinson? Ezekiel Porter introduced me to her back in 1858. I knew the woman—in fact, I *still* know her!"

Chapter 8

"You *know* Harriet Robinson?" Lizzie echoed Garrick Lloyd's words, staring in amazement.

The old man nodded vigorously. "My dear, Harriet is one of the bravest women I ever met. As a fighter for freedom, she is a legend."

"Why is it that I've never heard of this legend?" Dr. Walton wanted to know.

"But you have," Lloyd said. "Harriet made her way to Boston in late 1858. She didn't stay put very long, though. Instead, she risked her freedom to return to the South and lead other slaves along the Railroad."

"She was a conductor?" Walton said.

"One of the best," Lloyd told him. "She even married a man she helped to escape, and took his name—Stoneman."

Walton's mouth dropped open. "Harriet Stoneman? She was one of the best conductors in Tennessee and Kentucky. Even in the tense months right before the war, she smuggled dozens of runaways to freedom."

Lloyd nodded. "And during the war, she smuggled information. She was an important scout and spy. Make no mistake. She was—is—a true hero."

"And she's still alive," Walton marveled.

Garrick Lloyd barked a laugh. "Compared to me, she's a mere child—only seventy or so. We often exchange letters. Harriet had a rare master"—he turned to Lizzie—"your grandfather, I believe. He taught Harriet to read."

"That was Grandfather," Lizzie said proudly.

"I know I have Harriet's address somewhere." Lloyd reached over to a small table beside his chair and picked up a bell. The nurse came in and was ordered to search Lloyd's desk in his study. "Harriet decided to stay up north after the war. She's living in New York City these days." The nurse came back with a piece of paper. Lloyd read it, then passed it to Zachary Walton. "Here's where you'll find Harriet Stoneman."

The historian wanted to start for New York the next day, but Lizzie couldn't wait. She insisted they set off immediately. For the whole train ride down to New York she sat on the edge of her seat. At last, they reached Pennsylvania Station. Dr. Walton found a nice bench and sent the young folk out to hail a cab.

Lizzie was wide-eyed at the hustle and bustle of the big city. Neither Boston nor Washington had been this busy. But she grabbed Indy's hand and swam right into the crowds. Soon they had Dr. Walton and their luggage in a horse-drawn cab. They headed downtown to the address supplied by Garrick Lloyd.

"It's in an area called Greenwich Village, if my memory of New York is still good," Walton said. "Bleecker Street. That's right. There used to be a sizable Negro neighborhood in the area. Nowadays, I believe, immigrants have moved in. Italians, mainly."

Bleecker Street angled its way through a crowded neighborhood of dingy tenement buildings. When they stopped in front of the Stoneman address, their cab drew curious looks. "I don't think they see many hacks in these parts," Walton said, as he paid the fare.

Harriet Stoneman, it turned out, lived on the fifth floor of an old building. As they made their way up the last flight of steps, Lizzie said, "It must be hard for an old woman to keep going up and down all these stairs."

Dr. Walton didn't even answer. He was too busy trying to catch his breath as he climbed. Even his mustache looked wilted.

Indy wondered if he should suggest that the doctor rest. This adventure hadn't done him much good. Walton grimly continued up the stairs. He wanted to meet this legend.

They found themselves in a dim hallway. Seeing the faded and dirty walls, Indy said, "Looks like this place hasn't seen a coat of paint since the Civil War."

Lizzie led the way to the end of the hall. She knocked on a thin, wooden door. Seconds later, it opened to reveal a black woman in a plain cotton dress. Her hair was pure white, her face was wrinkled, and her back was bent. Yet she still moved briskly. She glanced from one face to the next.

"Well," she said in a surprisingly strong voice. "You folks from the moral uplift? Or the tenement commission, fixing to see that leak in the roof?"

Dr. Walton brushed a hand across his mustache, a little taken aback.

Lizzie stepped forward. "Mrs. Stoneman?" she asked.

"Who else?" Harriet Stoneman said. "You don't find many like me still in these parts."

"M-my name is Elizabeth Ravenall," Lizzie began, her voice trembling. At last, she was talking to Harriet, a woman who knew her grandfather. And this woman might hold the key to a fortune.

Harriet Stoneman looked at the girl more sharply. "Ravenall," she said, taking Lizzie's hand and drawing her inside. "And that drawl can only come from Carolina. Are you one of the Ravenalls from Ravenall Hall?"

"I'm afraid it's Clegg Hall now," Lizzie said. "But in Grandfather's—Ashley Ravenall's day—"

"Master Ashley," Harriet broke in. "That's what we always called him." She smiled. "Your grandfather was a good man, by his lights. I liked him. He really tried. You know, he always promised he'd set me free. When he died and that didn't happen, well, I ran away. And that was the real beginning of my life."

She looked curiously at Lizzie. "So, you don't want to save my soul or fix that leak. I expect you have something else in mind."

"I found my grandfather's journal last month. The last thing he wrote about was treasure—and how his children should ask you about it."

Indy leaned forward eagerly. This was it. Now Harriet would tell them the secret.

But the black woman gave Lizzie a blank

stare. "What should I know about— Oh . . ." Her eyebrows rose and she began to look embarrassed. "Treasure."

"You can tell me something?" Lizzie said eagerly.

"I don't see how it comes together," Harriet said. "I was only fifteen, an assistant cook in the kitchen." Her whole face changed as she thought back to those days. "I feel a little silly as I tell you this. Master Ashley often stopped by to talk with me. After his wife died, he would say that when he was gone, I'd have the thing I'd treasure most."

She looked at Lizzie, shaking her head. "Well, I was little more than a girl back then I sure didn't realize what he meant. There was this skillet in the kitchen, a big cast-iron thing. I thought it was the best thing on the whole plantation. And I called it Treasure."

"A skillet called Treasure?" Dr. Walton said. "Lizzie, could we have misunderstood what your grandfather was saying?"

Harriet Stoneman was still in the past. "Then Killer Clegg took over. He was as bad as your granddaddy was good, Lizzie. So I ran away, taking Treasure with me. After all, Master Ashley said I could have it after he was gone."

A smile softened her face as she remembered. "I knew so little in those days. But I finally understood what Master Ashley was trying to tell me. And I got the thing I most treasured—my freedom. Took a fight, but I got it."

Once again, the historian in Dr. Walton came out. "I'd like to talk to you about that fight, Mrs. Stoneman."

"Funny thing," Harriet Stoneman went on. "Treasure was an important part of it all. I got by in Tennessee and Kentucky as a wandering cook and washerwoman. Old Treasure cooked a lot of meals for slave-catchers and rebel soldiers. Who paid attention to a cook? I was almost invisible. That helped me move easy, to lead the runaways or carry messages."

Indy nodded, deep in thought. "Mrs. Stoneman, whatever happened to Treasure?"

"Why, I kept it. That skillet is just about indestructible. You know, it stopped a rifle ball outside Chattanooga."

Zachary Walton was happily scribbling away in his notebook. But Indy still frowned.

"Where is the skillet now?"

Harriet Stoneman shrugged. "It's hanging from a nail in the kitchen, over the stove."

"Do you think we could see it, ma'am? I think there's something more to Treasure than what you told us."

Chapter 9

Harriet Stoneman quickly led Indy into the kitchen. The room was small and cramped, but spotless. Over the stove was a collection of pots and pans. Indy didn't need to be told which one was Treasure.

The huge iron skillet had an area all to itself. It hung from an enormous nail driven into the wall, its old, blackened back standing out from the white paint.

Indy lifted Treasure down, marveling at the weight and heft of it. "I can see how you could stop a slave-catcher with one swing of this."

Harriet pointed to the inside of the pan. A big dent marred the surface of the iron. "That's where the bullet landed," she said. "Knocked me down. But all I had to show for it was a bruise. I was up and out of there as fast as my legs could take me."

Indy carefully examined the skillet. "Solid iron," he said. "Nothing comes off, so there's no place to hide anything." He studied the inside of the pan. Then he turned it over to examine the back. Holding the skillet up to the light of the kitchen, Indy stared hard. An excited gleam came into his eyes. "Ma'am, is there something here I can use to scour this?"

"You don't think it's clean enough?" Harriet asked, stung.

"Oh, it's clean on the inside—but I think the back may be hiding something."

"Well, you'll have some work ahead of you," the old woman said. "I cooked many a meal with that skillet. Take a heap of el-bow grease to get down to the iron again."

Indy scrubbed furiously, trying to cut through years of blackness. Just when he was about to give up, he caught the hint of a line.

He kept at it, scouring away at the back of the pan. Harriet Stoneman stood beside him, squinting at the lines that slowly came into view. "Miss Lizzie! Dr. Walton! Come in here and look at this!"

Soon they were all peering at what Indy had uncovered. "It looks like a map," Walton said.

"It's a floor plan of Clegg Hall!" exclaimed Lizzie.

"You mean Ravenall Hall," Harriet said. "This pan is fifty-five years old, after all." She looked hard at the intricate carving. "So long ago. Look, here's the kitchen. And what's this?"

She ran a finger to another mark etched into the iron. Lizzie and Indy strained their eyes. "Is that a cross?" Indy said.

"Looks like an 'X' to me. But where is it? What does it mean?" Lizzie wondered.

Harriet stared at the tiny scratches for a long time. "It's in Mrs. Ravenall's sewing room," she finally said. "So Master Ashley knew about it, after all."

"Knew what?" asked Lizzie.

"Mrs. Elizabeth had a special room built

onto the plantation house," Harriet explained. "It was a sewing room, but there was a closet in there that was only half as deep as it was supposed to be."

Lizzie Ravenall looked confused. "Why is that?"

"Child, the other half was for hiding people," Harriet answered.

"Hiding . . ." Lizzie's mouth sagged open, then snapped shut. "I'd heard tell that Grandma Elizabeth hated slavery and talked Grandfather into freeing the slaves. But— you're saying that she ran a station for the Underground Railroad?"

"A lot of people had secrets on that plantation," Harriet said. "Clegg had his rackets. Mrs. Elizabeth was hiding runaways. And now it seems that Master Ashley was up to something, too."

"And he used his wife's secret hiding place," Indy said.

"I can't believe it—my grandmother!" Lizzie said in wonder.

"Where do you think I learned about the Railroad?" Harriet asked. "From Mrs.

Elizabeth. I always thought Master Ashley might have approved of what she was doing. But it was against the law. And he was a mighty serious man about the law."

The old woman beckoned Lizzie close. "I'll tell you how to find that closet—and how to open the secret panel." Lizzie leaned over as Harriet Stoneman whispered in her ear.

Dr. Walton laughed. "You're going to keep secrets from the rest of us old campaigners?"

Harriet Stoneman smiled up at the historian. "I'll happily let you in on the secret," she said, "if your name is Ravenall."

She looked hard at Lizzie. "Now promise me, child. Don't tell anyone a word of what I told you."

"I promise," Lizzie said.

Several days later, Lizzie, Indy, and Dr. Walton were riding in a carriage through Clegg County. They'd taken a train to Charleston, then hired a buggy, driving slowly up toward Lizzie's hometown. It had been a long, tiring trip. But they were all too excited to care. This was the last lap to the treasure.

The final dash to Clegg Hall was planned for the cover of night. "We can be in and out before daybreak," Lizzie assured them. "Nobody lives in the old plantation house anymore. In fact, it's falling to ruin. Gideon Clegg ripped everything valuable out of the house. It's all in Clegg Manor. That's his new mansion, on the other side of his property. He wants people to forget the other house— and the Ravenalls who lived there."

Glancing over at her, Indy could see the proud lift of Lizzie's chin. She looked as if she was going off to war. But soon the war would be over—they'd have won. And what would happen between him and Lizzie then?

Dr. Walton held the reins, picking a careful route in the dim moonlight. The road, once graded and graveled, was filled with ruts. If they moved too fast, they stood a good chance of losing a wheel.

At last they reached the end of the road— a giant mud puddle in front of a pair of rusted iron gates. They were chained together and locked. But Indy waded through the muck, armed with a crowbar. He hardly needed to lever the chain away from the lock. It was so rusted, one good twist snapped it in two.

The hinges shrieked in protest as Indy pulled on gates that hadn't moved in decades. But Lizzie had told them that no one lived nearby. So who would hear?

They left the carriage inside the gates. Lizzie led the way across a hayfield that had once been a lawn.

"When I was little, I used to climb over the fence and play here," she said. "I know a way into the house."

By now they'd reached the front porch. Once, shining white pillars had towered up two stories to the roof. Now they were stained and discolored. In the moonlight, one pillar looked half eaten by termites.

"Right this way," Lizzie said confidently, stepping onto the porch. Her foot went right through a rotten board. If Indy hadn't been there to grab her, she'd have fallen flat on her face.

Moving more carefully now, they made their way to a set of French windows. Some of the glass was cracked. Other panes were missing. Lizzie reached through a gaping hole and twisted the handle.

The darkness inside seemed so thick, Indy could taste it. He lit the lantern he was carrying in his hand. The tiny flame sent weird shadows scampering on the walls. It was as if the old plantation's ghosts had leapt up from their sleep, surprised by the intruders.

Indy, Lizzie, and Dr. Walton found themselves almost tiptoeing toward the rear of the house. At last, they reached Mrs. Ravenall's sewing room.

Stepping inside, Lizzie peered at the back of the old skillet she carried. Then she looked around at the walls. From here on, she had only Harriet's fifty-year-old memories to go on. "Looks like the wallpaper was changed since Harriet was last here," she said.

"Let's just hope the closets weren't walled up," Indy muttered.

"Can't we get on with it?" Dr. Walton said, glancing at his watch.

Lizzie headed for the closet door nearest

the window. She pulled it open and stepped inside, pressing each corner of the back wall. They heard a loud *click*. Then a wooden panel fell outward. Indy caught it and eased it to the floor.

Lizzie took the lantern to light the secret room beyond.

It was empty.

The light flickered as Lizzie's hand began to shake. "I can't believe we went through all this—for nothing." She looked ready to cry.

"It's not over yet," Indy said, as he dropped to his knees on the floor of the hiding place.

"What are you looking for?" Lizzie asked.

"The floor back here is different from the floor in the front of the closet." Indy rested his hand on the floorboards, which had rotted through. Worms and grubs writhed away as he pulled the boards to pieces with his crowbar. "There's a space under here," he announced.

When the hole was large enough, everyone could glimpse what was hidden below—a large steel strongbox.

Indy worked to widen the hole, then pulled the strongbox out. "Looks pretty sturdy to me." He dragged the box from the closet. "I don't know if the crowbar will be enough to—"

The window beside them suddenly shattered. A man leapt through. The lantern light reflected off a pistol in his hand. Indy tried to jump to his feet, but the attacker knocked him sprawling.

Indy squinted up at the man—and groaned. It was Beau!

Then the beefy, red-haired thug jumped through the window. He stood covering Lizzie and Dr. Walton with another gun.

Finally, one more man climbed through, moving a little slower and more carefully. As he stepped into the pool of light, Indy could see he was an old man, with thin gray hair and spectacles. But the pistol in his hand was rock-steady.

"My name is Gideon Clegg," the man announced. "As if you didn't know, this house is mine." He gave them a nasty little smile. "That means anything found here belongs to me!"

Chapter 10

Indy came up off the floor with his fists clenched. He didn't care that those men had guns. If Dr. Walton could just distract them for a moment . . .

Then he realized that Zachary Walton had moved to stand with Gideon Clegg and the other two men. "Dr. Walton— What are you . . ." Indy's words trailed off as he realized the historian's action could mean only one thing.

"The good doctor works for me, you see," Clegg explained. "He has ever since my— ah—agents picked him up in Maryland."

"That's right, boy," Beau said with a grin. "But even with Walton's help, you gave me the slip once or twice. Good thing I picked you up again in Christiana."

Indy stared at him. "B-but how did you know we'd *be* in Christiana?" he finally managed to say. "How did you keep finding us?"

Beau's grin got bigger. "Let's just say I had a friend—a friend who'd go off to the telegraph office and let me know where you were going next."

Indy felt sick. Now he knew why Dr. Walton needed to sit down all the time. And to think Indy had worried when the historian sent him and Lizzie off by themselves. The man had been betraying them all the time!

Lizzie turned to Walton and stared at him pleadingly. "It can't be true," she whispered.

Zachary Walton just stood where he was, hanging his head. "I'm afraid it is," he finally managed to say. "They captured me and dragged me along in that wagon. First they threatened to beat me. Then—" He drew in a long breath. "Then they offered me money. A lot of money."

He looked up at Indy and Lizzie. "Please try to understand. I needed funds for my Civil War library. Here was a chance to get it started—to make my dream come true. I convinced myself that the end justifies the means. All they wanted was a telegram or two, telling them where we were heading. After New York, I thought we'd come here and find that Mr. Clegg had already taken the treasure. That would be the end of it."

"Doctor, come, come," Clegg said. "Miss Ravenall wouldn't tell you where the treasure was hidden. So I decided to let you three find it for me." He sneered at Dr. Walton. "I should think a historian would know all about dirty dealing through the ages."

"I expect *you* do," Indy said angrily.

Clegg shot him an annoyed glance. "Anyway, it's been a good business deal. I've invested a small amount in your silly library scheme, Doctor. But it's brought me a much larger return—the Ravenall fortune."

He stared greedily down at the strongbox. "Beau, get that lock off."

"Yes sir, Mr. Clegg." Beau pointed his pistol at the lock and squeezed the trigger. The crash of the shot was deafening in the small room. But the bullet did the job. The lock went flying to the far wall.

"Don't just stand there," Clegg said impatiently. "Open it."

Lizzie craned her neck, eager to see what her grandfather had left.

Beau cleared the hasp on the strongbox, then threw the top open. He pawed through the contents. "No gold or jewels, sir. Nor folding money." He glanced up at Clegg. Indy was amazed to realize that Beau was nervous. "Only thing in here is papers."

Clegg thrust out his hand. "Give them here." His eyes lit with excitement as he saw the papers clearly. "Stock certificates!"

But his excitement faded as he read on. "Bank of Atlanta—that was burned down when the Yankees marched through in '64. Natchez to Nashville Railroad—Yankees tore that up, too. Tredegar Ironworks—that was wrecked when the Yankees took Richmond in '65."

Clegg tossed the certificates back into the box. "That fool Ravenall invested in companies that don't exist anymore! They were all destroyed in the war. He must have spent thousands of dollars for those stocks. And now they're just worthless pieces of paper."

Clegg's face became ugly as he glared down at the strongbox. "You sure there's nothing else in there, Beau?"

"J-just this tied-up bundle," Beau stammered as he handed up the small package of papers.

Gideon Clegg quickly read through them. "These are ledger sheets from my pap's records," he said. "And these are letters from some lawyer in Charleston—Harkwood, I think it says."

"And they show how your father was cheating my grandfather," Lizzie said angrily. "He was supposed to be running the plantation. Instead, he was lining his pockets."

Clegg stared from the ledgers to the letters. "That's Pap's handwriting, all right. And if he sold all the stuff Harkwood bought, there's no record of it here."

"That Mr. Harlan, he musta been a sly one." The redheaded thug chuckled. "To think he was slickering those rich folk out of all sorts of money. Don't that beat—"

"Shut your stupid mouth!" Clegg roared, turning his pistol on his own man. The man's ruddy face went dead pale as he watched his boss. Clegg was livid with rage. "This is no joking matter. There's a note on these ledger pages from Ashley Ravenall. It says he's holding these pages as proof of theft. And it's dated September 13, 1858."

"That's the day Grandfather died," Lizzie said.

"I wonder if Harlan Clegg got wise that Ashley Ravenall was checking up on him," Indy said. "Suppose he found out about Mr. Ravenall's suspicions and plans—and ended them all with one blow?"

"A blow that knocked Grandfather off his horse and into the creek," Lizzie said grimly.

"You've got no proof of that." Clegg's voice was sharp.

"No, but there's proof enough in those papers that your father was a thief," Lizzie said. "Not that people ever doubted it—"

"Thinking something is true is one thing. Being able to prove it—that's another." Clegg's lips set in a thin line as he looked at the papers in his hand. "And this proof is trouble. It will make me a laughingstock, and it will make my pap out to be a murderer."

He turned hard eyes to Indy and Lizzie. "You know, you young 'uns have been an annoyance to me up to now. But now you're a downright danger. I can't let anyone leave this room unless they're on my side. And you two, you're never going to side with me, are you?"

Clegg rubbed a hand thoughtfully over his chin, then raised his pistol. "Well, from the look of it, this won't be the first time a Clegg killed a Ravenall who got in his way."

He clicked back the hammer on his gun. "And this being Clegg County, I don't see why a Clegg shouldn't get away with murder."

Chapter 11

Behind Clegg, Indy could see Zachary Walton standing and staring. The old historian's face was gray as ashes. He looked as if he'd aged ten years.

But Dr. Walton moved like a young man as he leapt to tackle Gideon Clegg. "You bought me as a spy," Walton yelled. "But all your money won't buy you a murder."

He and Clegg fell together in a noisy tangle of arms and legs. They rolled into Beau, knocking him over.

That left only the red-haired bruiser up and

ready to do anything. He stared slack-jawed, waiting for orders. Indy took advantage of the thug's hesitation to launch his own attack. One solid punch later, the big man was clutching his middle, his gun on the floor.

Lizzie picked up the gun and tossed it out the window.

Walton and Clegg rolled at the redhead's feet. They fought for control of Clegg's gun, yelling and thrashing. Neither seemed able to get the upper hand.

Indy turned to the last menace in the room—Beau. The black-bearded man was back on his feet. And his gun was aimed right at Indy.

"Nice try, boy," Beau said, his teeth gleaming against his dark whiskers. "But this time I end it for sure— *Yow!*"

Lizzie had just entered the battle, slamming Harriet Stoneman's skillet across Beau's shoulders. She swung with all her might. Beau staggered.

Indy leapt for the bearded thug, but Beau twisted aside, bringing his gun up to aim at Lizzie.

"No!!!" Indy screamed, trying to catch Beau's arm.

The gun went off.

Lizzie went down.

The whole world seemed to go red around the edges as Indy jumped on Beau. Anger made Indy unnaturally strong. He tore the gun from the man's grasp and threw it across the room. Then he began punching. He didn't stop until he realized someone was shaking him by the shoulders and yelling his name.

"Indy! Indy! Stop! You're going to kill him!"

"Wha—" The haze went away as Indy looked up. "Lizzie?" He glanced over to where he'd seen her fall. "I thought that he had killed—"

"Oh, he shot at me, all right," Lizzie said. "I'm afraid Beau put another dent in Treasure."

She held up the skillet. Sure enough, the back now had a huge crater with splattered metal around it.

"Gimme that gun!" a voice shouted from the floor. Indy whipped around. The red-haired thug was on his knees, his arms still

114

wrapped around his belly. Beau was knocked flat, unconscious. Clegg and Zachary Walton still rolled on the floor, fighting. "It's mine, ya old Yankee!" Clegg screamed, as Walton tried to twist the gun from his hand.

Then they rolled over the lantern.

Glass broke. The lamp oil spilled all over the floor and ignited. The wood burst into flame. Oh, great, Indy thought. Another fire. The back of Gideon Clegg's coat flared up. He lost his pistol as he tried to fight Walton and crush the flames on his back.

Indy leapt in, smothering the fire on Clegg. Walton got to his feet and held the man's pistol on him.

The blaze spread quickly. It was hopeless to try to stamp out the flames. "We've got to get out of here, pronto," Indy said. He prodded the redheaded strong-arm to his feet. "You and your boss carry Beau." With Walton guarding them, the two men picked up the unconscious thug.

Indy pushed them along, out onto the front porch. Then he realized someone was missing.

Lizzie hadn't come with them.

Flames were greedily eating up the rotted walls in the sewing room when Indy got back. Lizzie was paying no attention. She was busy trying to drag the old strongbox and the iron skillet to safety.

"Lizzie! Forget it! We've got to get out before this whole place goes up!"

She glared at him defiantly, a smudge of soot across one cheek. "I'm not leaving without Grandfather's box."

"But the stocks are all use—"

Indy's words were cut off by a rush of roaring flame. It swept up the wall and doorway behind him. A rotten beam gave way, falling from the ceiling. Blazing wreckage now blocked the door. Lizzie stared white-faced as Indy leapt over to her. But she still wouldn't let go of the strongbox.

"And you called *me* contrary," he said. Grabbing the strongbox and the skillet, he hurled them out the same window their attackers had entered through. Then he swept Lizzie up in his arms and ran for the opening. It was a desperate race against a wall of flame that blazed up to cut them off. Lizzie buried her face in Indy's shoulder as they leapt through. Then they were in the cool darkness outside.

Except for a couple of smoldering patches on their clothes, they were fine. Lizzie set to work gathering up the scattered contents of the box. Indy found Dr. Walton keeping a stern eye—and a pistol—on the prisoners.

"What do we do with them?" The doctor held the gun in a nervous grip.

"I saw some rope in our buggy," Indy said, running for the front gates. He came back with a coil of rope, then quickly went to work. In moments, Gideon Clegg and his strong-arm boys were tied up.

"They won't be going anywhere now," he said, satisfied. "I suppose we should report the fire."

"Looks pretty noticeable to me," Lizzie stared at the blazing mansion. The old plantation house had turned into an inferno. Flames were reaching the second floor and beyond, sending sparks and smoke up into the sky.

"I think Lizzie has a point," Dr. Walton

agreed, cupping a hand to his ear. In the distance they heard bells ringing. "Sounds like the fire company is on its way."

"Then we can leave them and get out of here," Indy said.

Lizzie nodded. "Let's head straight for town. The mail train will be coming by in a little while. We should be able to catch it."

Within half an hour, they were on a train to Charleston. The sun was coming up, but Dr. Walton lay back in his seat, dozing. He was totally exhausted after his battle with Gideon Clegg. Indy spent his time checking to see if anyone was following them. Lizzie calmly sorted through the contents of her grandfather's strongbox.

When she was done, she had three piles of slightly scorched papers on her seat.

"What's this?" Indy asked, turning from the window. They were out of Clegg County, at last. And it didn't look as if they were being followed.

"This pile here is proof that Harlan Clegg was a thief," Lizzie said, pointing to one batch of papers. "I'm going to drop that off with some people in Charleston. Gideon

Clegg has been high and mighty in Clegg County. But there are lots of folks in the state capitol who'll be happy to take him down a peg."

She put her hand on a thicker pile of papers. "These are Grandfather's investments in Confederate companies. Most of them, like the Tredegar Ironworks, were destroyed in the war. The rest have gone bankrupt, I'm afraid."

"They're all worthless?" Indy said. "I'm really sorry, Lizzie."

"Don't be," Lizzie said with a smile. "Grandfather didn't just invest in the South. Gideon Clegg would have discovered that if he'd really looked." She pointed to a third pile of papers. "These are all Yankee companies. Some of them did very well during the war. There's the Baltimore and Ohio Railroad, Colt Firearms, Du Pont Gunpowder, and a bunch of steel mills."

Lizzie tossed her head and smiled. "Looks like you don't have to worry about me."

Lizzie Ravenall returned to Washington a wealthy woman. Indy didn't see much of her for the next week, while she got her affairs in order. One of those pieces of business was donating money for a research library on the Civil War. Dr. Walton was very happy.

Indy wasn't happy, though. He'd come home to discover that his father had new plans and they didn't include Indy. Instead, Indy was to accompany a friend of his father's to Egypt. Egypt!

All too soon, Indy found himself saying good-bye to Lizzie. At least, he was *trying* to say good-bye.

"I—uh, I—Lizzie, I'm going to miss you something fierce," Indy finally blurted out. He knew his face had gone red once again.

Lizzie took his arm. "Indy, you've been a brave and true friend. I'll never forget you." She leaned forward, and her lips brushed his cheek. She'd kissed him!

"I bought you a present," she went on. "It seemed only fair, after all the trouble you went through on my account." She handed him a large, round box.

Indy opened it eagerly and found—a straw skimmer.

"I knew you'd like that. It's what you were wearing when we met,' Lizzie said. "Remember? It got crushed."

"Uh, thanks, Lizzie. Just what I need."

He stared at the hatbox and then at the girl's smiling face. Maybe leaving Washington wasn't such a bad idea. He'd miss Lizzie. But he wouldn't have to wear that silly hat. And who knows? Anything could happen in Egypt.

HISTORICAL NOTE

The Underground Railroad was a real thing. Many people risked their freedom and sometimes their lives to help slaves escape from the South.

How many slaves were saved? That's a question historians are still arguing about. Some claim as many as half a million slaves took Underground Railroad routes between 1820 and 1860. Others say there may have been as few as tens of thousands. No one knows. As a secret organization the UGRR, as it was known, kept no records.

Stories about slave escapes were very popular in northern newspapers. The tales of the slaves who escaped in disguise and by shipping themselves to freedom come from these accounts.

The main characters in the story are all made up. There was no Garrick Lloyd, but there was a William Lloyd Garrison, a fiery Boston editor who fought to abolish slavery. And although Harriet Stoneman is an imaginary character, there was a Harriet Tubman. She escaped from slavery but returned to the South on nineteen trips to bring her family and other slaves to freedom. She also served as a scout, spy, and nurse during the Civil War. Harriet Tubman was known as the Moses of her people. Oddly enough, she died in 1913—the year this story takes place.

TO FIND OUT MORE, CHECK OUT...

Long Journey Home: Stories from Black History by Julius Lester. Published by The Dial Press, 1972. Six stories based on the lives of slaves, including one unforgettable group who fled from their masters by walking into the sea.

Freedom Train: The Story of Harriet Tubman by Dorothy Sterling. Published by Doubleday, 1954. (Published in paperback by Scholastic.) An exciting biography of Harriet Tubman (who was the inspiration for the character Harriet Stoneman), from her childhood in slavery and her courageous escape to her days as conductor on the Underground Railroad and Civil War scout.

Flight to Freedom: The Story of the Underground Railroad by Henrietta Buckmaster. Published by Thomas Y. Crowell, 1958. A fascinating study of the Underground Railroad and the people who made it work.

Which Way Freedom? and *Out from This Place* by Joyce Hansen. Published by Walker, 1986 and 1988. Based on actual events, the first book tells how two slaves make a daring escape; the second book continues the story of their fight for freedom in the Civil War.

The War Between the States by Eric Wollencott Barnes. Published by McGraw-Hill, 1959. A dramatic history of the Civil War: its causes, battles, people, and effects. Maps, illustrations.

SHARE THE ADVENTURE!

Follow the adventures of Young Indiana Jones through the pages of The Official Lucasfilm Fan Club Magazine. Each issue has exclusive features, behind-the-scene articles and interviews on the people who make the *Indiana Jones* films as well as *Star Wars!* Plus there are special articles on the Disney theme-park spectaculars, Lucasfilm Games as well as Industrial Light & Magic — the special effects wizards! You can also purchase genuine collectors items through the club's official catalog such as theater one-sheets, toys, clothing, as well as products made exclusively for members only!

YOUR MEMBERSHIP INCLUDES:

A fantastic 10th anniversary *Empire Strikes Back* Membership Kit including:

- Exclusive *ESB* One-Sheet (originally created for *ESB,* but never produced!)
- Embroidered Fan Club Jacket Patch!
- Two *ESB* 8x10 full color photos!
- *Star Wars* Lives bumper sticker!
- Welcome letter from George Lucas!
- Full-color Membership Card!

PLUS:

- One-year subscription to the quarterly full-color Lucasfilm Magazine!
- Cast and crew fan mail forwarding!
- Classified section (for sale, wanted & pen pals section!)
- Science Fiction convention listing!
- And more!

NEW

JOIN FOR ONLY $9.95